A WILD AND WOOLLY NIGHT

By **Lorraine Lynch Geiger**

Illustrated by **Sharon Vargo**

The RGU Group • Tempe, Arizona

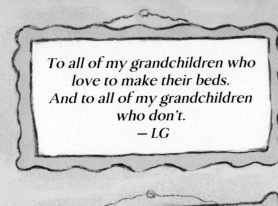

*To all of my grandchildren who
love to make their beds.
And to all of my grandchildren
who don't.*
— LG

*For my wild and woolly boys ...
Ryan, Scott, Craig & Kevin*
— SV

The illustrations were rendered in colored pencil and painted in acrylic on Strathmore Bristol.
The text type was set in Danmark. The display type was set in Oliver. Composed in the United States of America.
Graphic layout by Adriana Patricia De La Roche. Production supervision by Laura Bofinger.

Text copyright © 2007 by Lorraine Lynch Geiger. Illustrations copyright © 2007 by Sharon Hawkins Vargo.

First impression. Printed in Singapore.

Library of Congress Cataloging-in-Publication Data

Geiger, Lorraine Lynch.
    A wild and woolly night / by Lorraine Lynch Geiger ; illustrated by Sharon Vargo.
        p. cm.
    Summary: Every time Phillip changes his bedspread, different animals invade his
bedroom, from starfish to otters, leopards, and bears.
    ISBN-13: 978-1-891795-25-1 (hard cover)
    ISBN-10: 1-891795-25-2 (hard cover)
    [1. Animals--Fiction. 2. Coverlets--Fiction. 3. Bedtime--Fiction.
4. Stories in rhyme.]   I. Vargo, Sharon ill. II. Title.
PZ8.3.G274Wi 2007
[E]--dc22   2006028879

www.theRGUgroup.com
10 9 8 7 6 5 4 3 2 1 (sc)

When Phillip made his bed one day,
With stars of blue and white,
He found that he could hardly wait
To climb in bed that night.

"These stars will help me go to sleep.
I'll keep these stars," he said.
But when he went to bed he found ...

Six starfish there instead.

"What! Starfish in my bed?" he cried.
"Now how did these get here?
Why now I'll never fall asleep.
With starfish everywhere!"

Instead, he found a purple spread
With tiny polliwogs.
But when he climbed back into bed ...

They all grew into frogs.

"I cannot sleep with frogs," he sighed.
"Now this is just too much.
These frogs will make a lot of noise
And hop and croak and such."

Then Phillip stated, "I know what!
I'll try a spread with lines."
But when he got back into bed ...

He found nine porcupines.

Young Phillip stared in disbelief.
"How can I sleep with quills?
They're sharp and pointy," Phillip said.
"Just looking gives me chills.

"I know," he said. "A spread of shells.
Just maybe, that will help."

But soon a playful otter came
Along with piles of kelp.

"Just what do I do now?" Phil groaned.
"Are otters ever still?
I'll never get to sleep," he scowled.
"I *know* I never will.

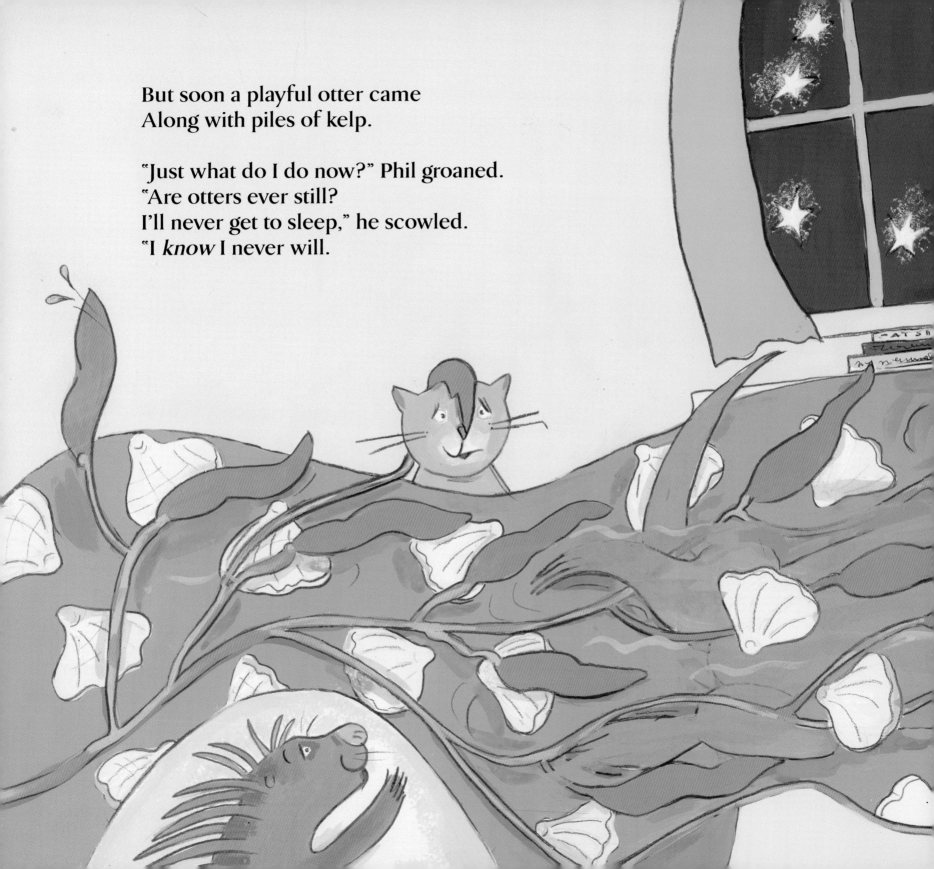

"Though maybe I just might doze off
With scenes of jungle trees."
But soon his room was overrun ...

With swinging chimpanzees.

"These chimps are really troublesome,"
Said Phillip, quite distressed.
"I need to find a different spread
So I can get some rest.

"Perhaps," he said, "The problem is
I need a different size."

But, right away, three great horned owls
Flew in to socialize.

"Oh no! Not owls. I don't want owls.
I don't want owls at all!
I cannot fall asleep with owls.
Not even if they're small."

Then Phillip said, "I'll switch to pink.
To see if I can doze."
But when he peeked from underneath ...

Flamingoes stood in rows.

"What's this?" he yelled. "Flamingoes now?
Flamingos in my bed?
I need to find a spread that's right.
And not just *any* spread.

"Instead of pink, I think I'll try
Some black and some white shapes."

But then two pandas wandered in
While munching on some grapes.

"What? Pandas in my room, as well?
It goes from bad to worse."
Poor Phillip sighed with discontent,
"I'll *never* sleep, of course.

"I must be careful what I choose.
A spread with spots, perhaps."

But soon two leopards bounded in
And lay down for their naps.

"I can't have leopards in my room,"
Cried Phillip in despair.
"There's just no way that I can sleep
With leopards napping here.

"I'll try a comforter," he said,
"With stripes of black and white."

But zebras leaped upon his bed
And bounced all through the night.

"These things are huge! Too huge for me!
I cannot sleep with these.
I'd never even get one wink!
Won't someone move them, *PLEASE?*

"A swampy spread could make me sleep,"
Said Phillip, turning in.

But soon, four smiling crocodiles
Crawled right past Phillip's chin.

"Now how did crocs arrive?" he said.
"These creatures are not nice.
Before I choose another spread
I'll think, not once, but twice.

"I know. Some stripes and polka dots
Will stop this mean riffraff."
But when he closed his eyes that night ...

In swaggered a giraffe.

"No! No! Get out of here!" he said.
"And please don't make one peep.
Be quiet all of you in here!
You *must* all let me sleep.

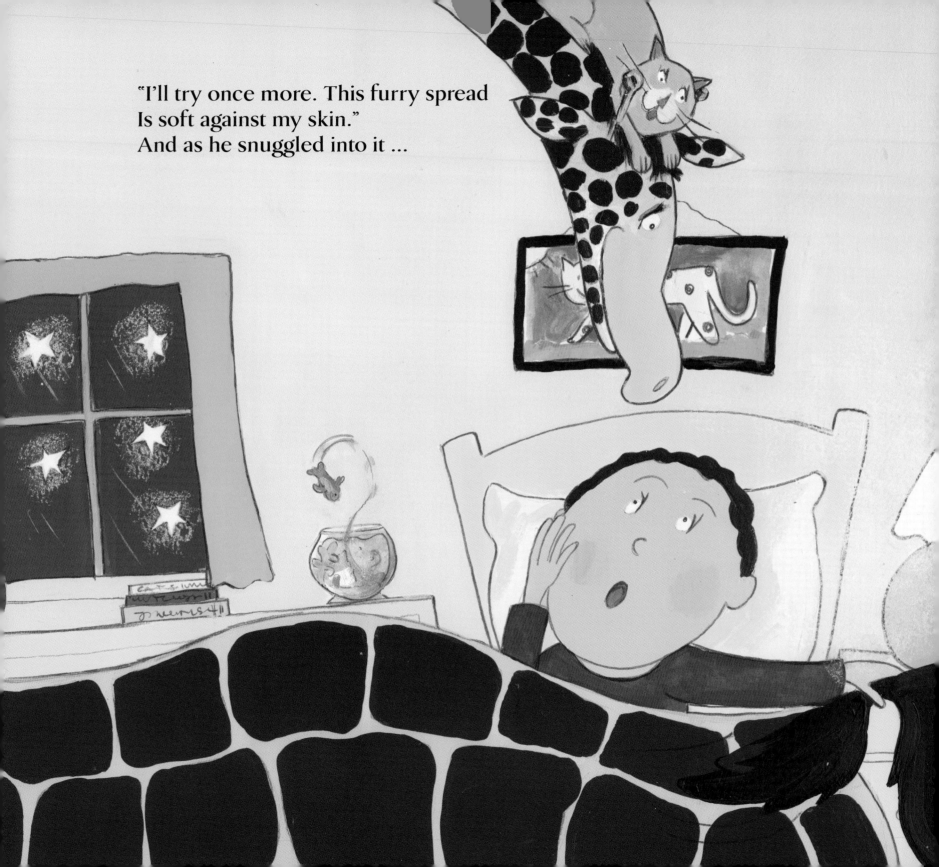

"I'll try once more. This furry spread
Is soft against my skin."
And as he snuggled into it ...

A black bear straggled in.

He climbed on Phillip's crowded bed
And curled into a ball.
And yawned a sleepy black bear yawn
As wide as it was tall.

Then, one by one, the porcupines
All started yawning, too.
And after that, the great horned owls
Stopped asking *Whoo? Whoo? Whoo?*

The zebras and the tall giraffe
All leaned against the walls.
The starfish, frogs, and otter, too,
Reclined on basketballs.

And soon the pandas and the crocs
Began to fall asleep.
The leopards and the chimpanzees
All snoozed without a peep.

They all curled up in corners, and
On dressers, and in shoes.
Some leaned against the closet doors
And all began to snooze.

Then, sleepy Phillip yawned a yawn
As wide as it was deep.
And then he curled up with the bear ...

And soon was sound asleep.